D1192429

Copyright © 1999 by Nord-Süd Verlag AG, Gossau Zürich, Switzerland
First published in Switzerland under the title *Das neue Schwesterchen*
English translation copyright © 1999 by North-South Books Inc.

First published in the United States, Great Britain, Canada,
Australia, and New Zealand in 1999 by North-South Books,
an imprint of Nord-Süd Verlag AG, Gossau Zürich, Switzerland.

Distributed in the United States by North-South Books Inc., New York.

Library of Congress Cataloging-in-Publication Data is available.
A CIP catalogue record for this book is available from The British Library.

ISBN 0-7358-1056-7 (trade binding)
1 3 5 7 9 TB 10 8 6 4 2
ISBN 0-7358-1057-5 (library binding)
1 3 5 7 9 LB 10 8 6 4 2
Printed in Belgium

For more information about our books,
and the authors and artists who create them,
visit our web site: http://www.northsouth.com

Gerda Marie Scheidl

Tommy's New Sister

Illustrated by Christa Unzner

Translated by J. Alison James

North-South Books · New York · London

Tommy had always lived with his mother and father and his best friend, Muffin the dog. He was very happy. Then along came a baby. Her name was Wendy. And Wendy stayed—for weeks and weeks!

"Doesn't she look pretty in her new outfit?" asked Tommy's father one day.

"She's still bald!" Tommy said.

"You didn't have any hair either, when you were a baby," said his mother.

She picked up the baby. Tommy wanted to be picked up too.

"Tommy," said his mother, "you're our big boy now. Tell you what, you can help me give her a bath. Would you like that?"

"No," said Tommy defiantly. "I'm busy."

He went to his room.

He didn't want to be a big boy.

Muffin followed Tommy to his room. They flopped down in the play corner.

"Want to hear the story of Peter Pan, Muffin?" Tommy asked. "The little girl in the story is named Wendy, just like that baby."

"Woof!" said Muffin. She wagged her tail and listened as Tommy told the story.

"... so then," Tommy continued, "Tinkerbell sprinkled fairy dust over Wendy, and they flew away together."

Muffin was asleep.

"Hey!" Tommy said, prodding Muffin. "We can sprinkle fairy dust on the baby! Then she'll fly away to Neverland."

"Woof," said Muffin.

Tommy made a bowl of fairy dust out of flour and cocoa powder and sugar. But when he sprinkled it on the baby, she didn't fly away. She started shrieking. Tommy quickly tried to clean up the fairy dust. Too late! His mother was already there.

"Tommy! What are you doing? Look at this mess!"

"I didn't mean to make a mess," Tommy said, "I just wanted her to fly away to Neverland like Wendy does in *Peter Pan*. Then things would be the way they used to be, and..."

Tommy's mother smiled and drew Tommy close to her. "Our Wendy can't fly, and magic things like that only happen in fairy stories. Please, Tommy, don't try anything like that again."

Tommy nodded.

The telephone rang. Tommy ran to get it.

It was Granny. "Hello, Tommy," she said. "I wanted to visit you this weekend, but unfortunately I've caught a cold."

"Oh, no," Tommy said. He liked Granny's visits.

"I'm terribly sad," said Granny, "because I won't be able to see you and little Wendy. I'll bet she's changed a lot since the last time I saw her."

Granny shouldn't be sad. Tommy knew just what to do.

"I can send her to you," he said.

Granny laughed and said, "How kind of you to offer."

"You could keep her as long as you like," Tommy said.

"But won't you miss her, Tommy?"

"It's okay," he said, and hung up the phone quickly. He was happy now. The baby was going to Granny's.

Tommy found the box with air holes in it. It was the box Muffin came home in when she was just a tiny puppy. The baby was tiny too. She should fit just right.

But when Tommy picked her up and tried to put her in the box, she started to howl. She sounded like a fire engine.

Tommy's mother came running.

"Tommy!" she cried. "What on earth are you doing?"

"I'm sending the baby to Granny," Tommy said. "Granny really wants to see her."

Stunned, Tommy's mother flopped into the nearest chair. She was speechless.

"You must be out of your mind!" Tommy's father was furious. "You can't put a baby in a box and ship her off."

"Why not?"

"Why not? Because it is much too dangerous."

"No it isn't," cried Tommy. "No it isn't." He burst into tears and ran to his room. He was really angry.

Sniffling, Tommy crawled under his bed. He wanted to be invisible. Muffin crawled in after him.

Now his mother and father were both angry with him. That wasn't what he wanted. He only wanted them to love him again.

"What can I do, Muffin?" Tommy asked.

"Woof," said Muffin. Muffin was no help.

But Tommy had an idea.

He picked up everything in his room, all by himself, without being told.

Muffin helped. She fetched the wooden blocks and the teddy bear.

Tommy put his books in a neat row on the shelf.

He put the train on its track.

Now his room looked nice! His mother would be pleased.

"Come in here!" he called to her. "I want to show you something!"

"Not right now," his mother replied.

"Right now!" shouted Tommy, and he ran to find her.

Tommy's mother was holding Wendy in her arms.

Tommy ran back to his room in a temper. He messed up his nice neat room. He had never been so angry with anyone in his life. He hated that baby! He wanted to shoot her to the moon! That made him laugh, Wendy rocking in a moon cradle.

Tommy listened. Wendy was crying now. Crybaby.

Why wasn't anyone going to her?

Tommy went to the kitchen and listened. Nobody was there. Everything was quiet except for the baby crying.

Where was his mother?

Where was his father?

Wendy cried and cried.

Something squeezed in Tommy's stomach. "My sister shouldn't be left alone to cry," he muttered. "She's just a little baby." He ran into Wendy's room. Her face was all red from crying.

"Shush, shush," Tommy whispered to her.

She kept on crying.

He touched her cheek. Impulsively he stuck his finger in her mouth.

Wendy grabbed his hand and sucked hard on his finger. She looked right at Tommy and stopped crying.

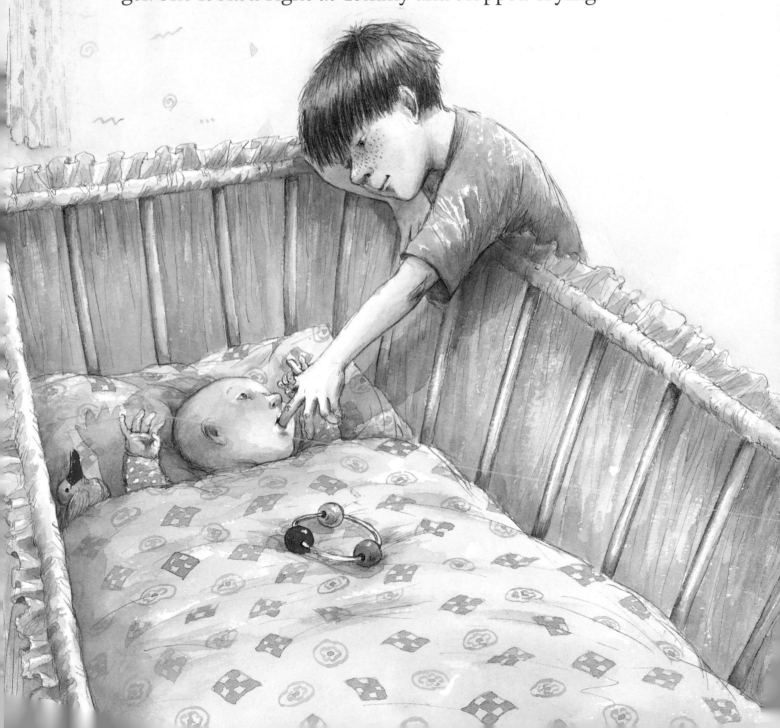

"Look at what a wonderful big brother you have, Wendy," Mama said, coming into the room. She gave Tommy a big hug, and kissed his head.

Tommy beamed. Suddenly he was proud to be Wendy's big brother. He wanted to keep her forever, his own little sister.

Daddy got the camera out to take a family picture. Wendy sat in Tommy's lap, and their mother sat with both of them. Muffin lay down beside them all.

"Woof," said Muffin. She was part of the family too.